LAYLA and the BOTS

HAPPY PAWS

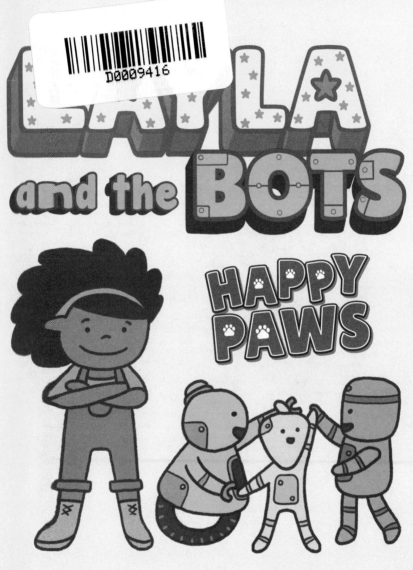

written by
Vicky Fang

illustrated by
Christine Nishiyama

BRANCHES

SCHOLASTIC INC.

For my rock stars, Taso & Leo –VF
To Declan. For everything. –CN

Text copyright © 2020 by Vicky Fang
Illustrations copyright © 2020 by Christine Nishiyama

Library of Congress Cataloging-in-Publication Data

Names: Fang, Vicky, author. | Nishiyama, Christine, illustrator.
Title: Happy paws / by Vicky Fang ; illustrated by Christine Nishiyama.
Description: First edition. | New York, NY : Branches/Scholastic Inc., 2020.
| Series: Layla and the Bots | Summary: While Layla and her three Bots
(Beep, Boop, and Bop) are setting up for their rock band's performance,
she gets some bad news, Happy Days Amusement Park is closing; Layla thinks
she has the perfect solution: turn the place into an amusement park for
dogs—but the new rides have to pass a safety inspection before Happy Paws
Amusement Park can open.

Identifiers: LCCN 2019007650 | ISBN 9781338582895 (pbk. : alk. paper) |
ISBN 9781338582901 (hardcover : alk. paper)
Subjects: LCSH: Dogs—Juvenile fiction. | Amusement parks—Juvenile fiction. | Amusement
rides—Juvenile fiction. | Robots—Juvenile fiction. | CYAC:
Dogs—Fiction. | Amusement parks—Fiction. | Amusement rides—Fiction. |
Robots—Fiction.
Classification: LCC PZ7.1.F3543 Hap 2020 | DDC [Fic]—dc23 LC record available at
https://lccn.loc.gov/2019007650

10 9 8 7 6 5 4 3   21 22 23 24

Printed in the U.S.A. 40
First edition, May 2020

Illustrated by Christine Nishiyama
Edited by Rachel Matson and Katie Carella
Book design by Maria Mercado

TABLE OF CONTENTS

1
MEET LAYLA AND THE BOTS

This is Layla. She is an inventor. And a rock star.

These are the Bots.

BEEP

BOOP

BOP

They are part of Layla's crew.

Layla and the Bots live in an ordinary town called Blossom Valley.

But ever since Layla built her Bots, her life is anything but ordinary.

4

You see, Layla and the Bots are famous!
They play awesome rock music together
and perform in all sorts of cool places.

And when they're
not playing music,
they're putting their
invention skills to work.

TAP!
TAP!

Whenever Layla and the Bots get together, awesome things happen.

2
NOT-SO-HAPPY DAYS

On Monday morning, Layla and the Bots unpack their band gear at the Happy Days Amusement Park. They have a big show in five days!

What? But why?

People have stopped coming to the park. It's been slow for a year. I just can't stay open.

Wade seems so sad. He keeps talking, but Layla doesn't hear him. Close Happy Days? She has so many memories from the park!

After Wade leaves, Layla tells the Bots the bad news.

Wade is closing Happy Days!

How come?

Warghh!

BEEP. Happy Days is my favorite—

Layla cuts Beep off.

I feel the same way, which is why we are not going to let it happen. We have to save Happy Days! Are you with me?

Yes!

3
FOLLOW THAT BARK

Layla and the Bots visit town.

THIS FRIDAY!
LAYLA + THE BOTS
AT HAPPY DAYS

THIS FRIDAY!
LAYLA + THE BOTS
AT HAPPY DAYS

It's time to investigate. We have to figure out why people have stopped going to Happy Days. Where are they going instead?

Suddenly, they hear something.

BARK!
BARK!

What is that?

BEEP. Sounds like barking.

But where are the dogs?

They follow the barking sounds.

The town dog park is overflowing with people—and dogs!

So <u>this</u> is where everybody is going for fun now!

Woof-doggies!

BLOSSOM VALLEY DOG PARK

Beep, how many dog owners are there in Blossom Valley?

BEEP. There are four thousand homes in Blossom Valley. Half of the households own a dog. That's two thousand dog owners.

Two thousand!?

Wow-zees!

Layla thinks back to when the amusement park first opened.

Happy Days used to have a doggy day care.

HAPPY DAYS
DOG CARE

BEEP. That closed twelve months ago.

It's true, the dogs were bored there. And the <u>whole</u> amusement park has to be fun!

This gives Layla an idea.

FOR THE DOGS!

Layla and the Bots rush back to Happy Days. Layla tells Wade about all the people they saw at the town dog park.

You see, people don't want to leave their dogs at home. They want to bring their dogs <u>with</u> <u>them</u> to have fun!

Layla grins.

I agree! But what if Happy Days could be an amusement park that is fun for people _and_ dogs? There could be actual rides and games for _dogs_!

Wade scratches his head.

But how could we do that? We'd have to re-design the entire park. I don't think it's possible.

Layla looks at the Bots.

Maybe we could help.

I don't know, Layla.
It's a pretty huge and wild idea.

TUNNEL OF MYSTER

Layla thinks he might be right. But she
has to do <u>something</u>.

Inside, Layla's stomach is flipping.
Can she really do this?

5

PUPPY LOVE

The next day, Layla and the Bots sit at the ice cream shop in town. Layla has her notebook and a pencil.

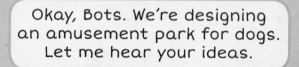

Okay, Bots. We're designing an amusement park for dogs. Let me hear your ideas.

They head back to the dog park to investigate some more.

They see dogs eating treats,

dogs playing ball,

and dogs getting their tummies rubbed.

One fluffy dog is rolling in the mud.

A brown dog is chewing on a squeaky toy.

Two spotted dogs are chasing a squirrel.

Soon, Layla is sketching ideas in her notebook. Beep, Boop, and Bop sketch too.

By the end of the day, Layla and the Bots have two dozen ideas.

BEEP. We have twenty-four ideas.

Layla squints at the mess of papers.
How is she going to choose?

6

DIAMONDS IN THE RUFF

On Wednesday morning, Layla has a plan.
She hands a stack of ideas to each Bot.

We need to get feedback on our ideas.
Let's share them with the dog owners
to hear what they think.

Just then, a woman with a shaggy dog runs up.

Hey, I thought of something else! My dog really loves to stick her head out the car window.

Mine too!

Same here.

Hmm . . .

Layla grabs her notebook and sketches out a new idea.

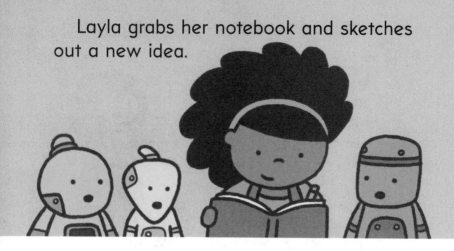

She shows the dog owners.

Yes!

Amazing!

So cool.

Make that six great ideas!
Bots, it's time to go build.
TUMMY LOVE MACHINE!
Whoop-yay!

7

BEEP BOOP BOP

Layla and the Bots are ready to put their plan into place.

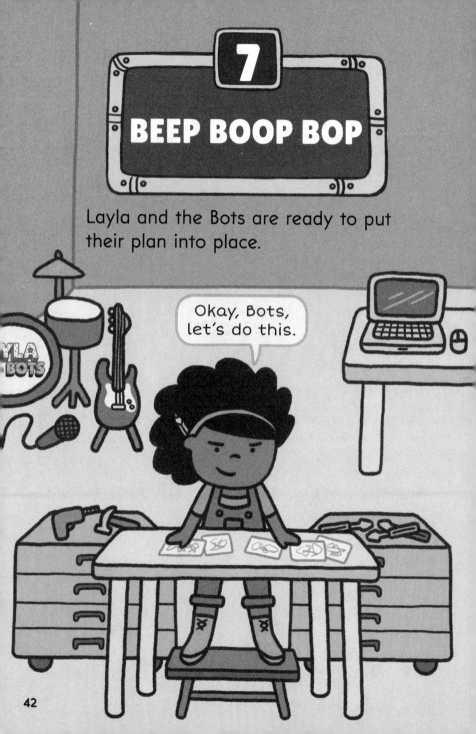

Okay, Bots, let's do this.

Beep lays out the drawings.

Boop prepares her tools.

Bop practices karate while his computers boot up.

First, Beep checks what dogs like to eat.

Boop builds the Pick-a-Treat machine.
It is filled with bones, sausages, and
doggy treats.

Bop codes the buttons to deliver the right food.

Next, Beep picks out petting styles.

Boop builds the Tummy Love machine.

It can rub,

pat,

or scratch.

Bop tinkers to get the settings just right.

```
ScratchDog(dogHeight)
{if (dogHeight>20
  ->scratchBelly,
  else scratchBack;}
```

import
#good
boy
function

TUMMY LOVE

Nice work.

Then they build the Flying Ball Pit,

the Squeaky Toy Chase,

SQUEAK!

SQUEAK!

and the Rub-a-Dub Mud Slide.

They even build a Breezy Car-Coaster!
Beep looks up all kinds of car models.

Boop builds windows
so the dogs can stick
their heads out.

Bop makes sure the cars speed up and
slow down at the right times.

TAP!
TAP!

On Thursday night, Layla and the Bots take their brand-new dog rides to Happy Days. Tomorrow they will show them to Wade.

The dogs will love this roller coaster!

LOADING DOCK

BREEZY CAR-COASTER

But as Layla lies in bed, she worries . . . Will it be enough to save the park?

8
A TOO–BIG SNAG

On Friday morning, Layla and the Bots show Wade their new inventions.

Layla and the Bots dance their way toward the stage.

See you at the show!

They start tuning their instruments. But then . . .

Wade runs over to them.
He looks worried.

We've got a problem. The safety inspector
won't approve the Breezy Car-Coaster.
She says the windows are too big and
a small dog could fall out.

Too big?

Uh-ohs!

56

Layla slumps down on the edge of the stage.

Wade, I'm so sorry I let you down. I let us _all_ down.

No, Layla. You did your best. Maybe Happy Paws just wasn't meant to be.

BEEP. This challenge was just too big.

Yep, wrong size!

Suddenly, Layla looks up.

And Bop, you come with me. We've got less than two hours until the park opens!

Layla and the Bots work together until the Breezy Car-Coaster is fixed.

9

BEST IN SHOW

The safety inspector looks over the new Breezy Car-Coaster.

Wow, I can't believe it. How did you fix the Car-Coaster?

Easy. Bop and I wrote code to change the size of the window. Let me show you what I mean.

Layla shows Wade the updated plans for the Breezy Car-Coaster.

BREEZY CAR-COASTER

When a dog steps up to the loading dock, the camera measures its size.

CAMERA

Then the code adjusts how far the window opens.

If small dog -> window up high
If medium dog -> window half open
If big dog -> window down low

Wade opens the park. Everyone loves Happy Paws!

Soon, it's time to rock out!

69

It was Layla and the Bots' best show ever.

DESIGN AND BUILD YOUR OWN

YOU'LL NEED THE FOLLOWING ITEMS:

- 5 or more cardboard tubes
- 5 or more plastic bottles
- 1 large piece of cardboard
- Scissors
- Glue
- Duct tape
- Marble or small ball
- Paper cup (optional)

NOTE: Many of these items can come from your
recycling bin! Be sure to have an adult
clean out the bottles and remove any
staples from the cardboard.

STEP 1. BUILD THE BASE

- Tape the bottles to your cardboard base.
  These are the pillars for your roller coaster.

TIP: Line up your pillars
from tallest to shortest.
Keep them close enough
that your cardboard
tubes can connect them.

STEP 2. BUILD THE TRACK

- Cut your cardboard tubes in half length-wise
  to create pieces for your track.
- Place your tracks to connect the
  pillars and tape them into place.

ROLLER COASTER!

STEP 3. TEST AND FIX

- Test out your roller coaster! Place your marble at the top and watch it zoom down the track.
- Does your marble fall off? Or get stuck? It's time to problem solve! Add, move, or take away from your design to make it work.

TIP: You can add a cup to the end of the track to catch your ball.

STEP 4. ROCK OUT!

- Have fun! Experiment with different-sized balls, track designs, and pillar heights to see what happens.
- Give your ride a fun name, and draw a picture of your design.
- Decorate your roller coaster with paint, glitter, and anything else you'd like!

HOW MUCH DO YOU KNOW ABOUT HAPPY PAWS?

Reread page 11. How does Layla feel when Wade tells her that Happy Days has to close? How do you know she feels this way?

Happy Days used to have a doggy day care, but it closed. What happened to the park <u>after</u> the doggy day care closed?

Layla and the Bots visit the dog park to learn what dogs do for fun. What do they see at the park? What ideas come out of this visit?

The safety inspector won't approve the Breezy Car-Coaster. What problem did she find? How do Layla and the Bots fix the problem?

Imagine you get to build an amusement park for pets! What animals would visit your park? What rides would you make for them? Draw and label a map of your park!

ABOUT THE CREATORS

VICKY FANG is a product designer who invents things like cars that talk to each other and robots you can build at home. She has never designed a roller coaster for dogs, but she did help her boys design a terrarium for their pet darkling beetle! Vicky lives in California with her husband and kids. LAYLA AND THE BOTS is her first early chapter book series.

CHRISTINE NISHIYAMA is an artist who draws all kinds of things in her sketchbook. She's passionate about helping others make art and teaches students online. Christine lives in North Carolina with her husband and her dog, Oni. Christine is also the author and illustrator of the picture book WE ARE FUNGI.

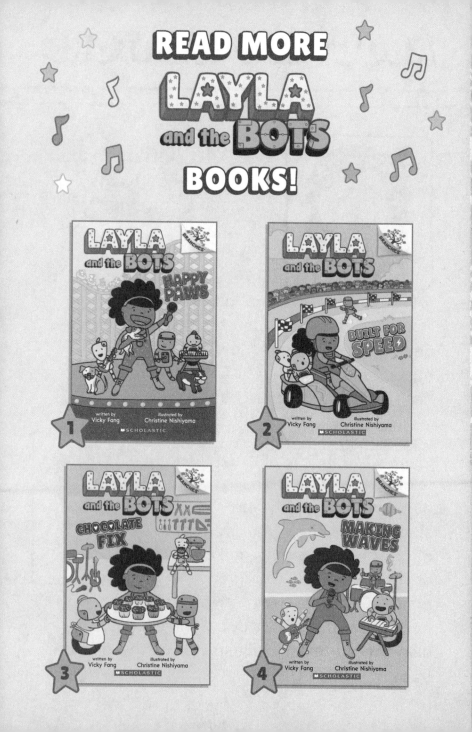